Steven is originally from Washington state. For several years he performed as a musician, then moved over to the cruise industry, where he worked for twenty-three years as a cruise director, lecturer, and art director. After retiring from the cruise ships, he moved to Las Vegas, where he worked for several years as a gallery director on the Las Vegas strip. Now, in his senior years, he enjoys working as a gallery director for a new art gallery on Cannery Row in Monterey, California.

Steven Lundquist

WHAT'S LOVE GOT TO DO WITH IT?

AUSTIN MACAULEY PUBLISHERS™

LONDON • CAMBRIDGE • NEW YORK • SHARJAH

Ordering Information
Quantity sales: Special discounts are available on quantity purchases by corporations, associations, and others. For details, contact the publisher at the address below.

Publisher's Cataloging-in-Publication data
Lundquist, Steven
What's Love Got to Do with It?

ISBN 9798891554948 (Paperback)
ISBN 9798891554955 (ePub e-book)

Library of Congress Control Number: 2024900077

www.austinmacauley.com/us

First Published 2024
Austin Macauley Publishers LLC
40 Wall Street, 33rd Floor, Suite 3302
New York, NY 10005
USA

mail-usa@austinmacauley.com
+1 (646) 5125767

Synopsis

The Poet of Auschwitz

A man's love for his wife defines his very existence, as the tragedy of Auschwitz unfolds in his life and the life of his family. His every thought is fueled by the desire for revenge, until finally, with the help of his wife's spirit, he begins to discover the true meaning of life and love evolving from deep within himself.

Las Vegas

Las Vegas at its worst. An honest emotion could only appear from a great distance, for Las Vegas itself is devoid of humanity. Or is it? Would it be possible to create a tinge of humanity within the all-encompassing circuit boards of gambling, intoxication, and spurious sexual glorification? The answer is surprising and unexpected; for God's love will find a way, through the voice of a brutalized young woman, even within the hopelessness of a dark and terrifying world.

Elegy

This reveals the evolution, with flashbacks, of a young woman who has been working for the past two years as a fashion designer in Manhattan. It begins with the realization that she's being called by her Archangel, Michael, to move on to the next step in her development as an angel. She's living in confusion, with only vague memories of a previous life. But eventually, she'll recall her past, and begin to fulfill her destiny in a heroic showdown with the devil.

The Secret to Happiness

This piece is all dialogue, and there's nothing "happy" about it. It starts with a broken-down, alcoholic detective, sitting behind the desk in his office as he talks to a visitor (who we find out later is "death"), when a beautiful young woman suddenly walks in. The idea was to convey the feeling of a film noir movie from the '40s. It barely mentions the word love, and only in an offhanded way. Yet perhaps the absence of love can sometimes be a statement about love.

The Poet of Auschwitz

"I never expected to live this long. Somehow I just keep waking up, but always with you on my mind. The sky is so incredibly beautiful, my love. It's the first thing you'll see when you open your eyes in heaven. Stars flowing through the mist of our forgotten dreams. Sunlight melting the tears of this brutal, overwhelming despair.

"I remember the first time I saw you. The spirit of love and laughter danced across your face. You were so happy to be alive. What did you know that the rest of us could never have imagined? What was the secret that you carried with you to the grave?

"I have a strange feeling that it was your sense of freedom that made you so alive, a freedom that abandoned us all so long ago. All that I have now is the joy of holding your smile in a corner of my mind that they can never touch.

"Why did it suddenly become a sin to be who we are? We've lived glorious, noble lives. For centuries we've shared the joy of our artistic heritage with the world. Music of surpassing beauty. Mind-boggling paintings infused with the color of our unique understanding of the world around us. We're the guardians of the soul, not the vile, repulsive creatures that they've painted us to be.

"Can't they see that we're all simply an extension of God's hand? An implausible truth created in a moment of divine speculation? An experiment now gone so horribly wrong within these chambers of eviscerated souls?

"The devil stands over us, my love. His cruelty is boundless. But revenge is my salvation.

"I'll come at them with a ferocity unknown to these little thimbles that pass for rational minds. They'll know the true meaning of terror. I promise."

On a quiet evening early in the spring of 1945, a warm wind descended on the house of Himmler: a palatial, seventeen-room villa on the outskirts of Recife, a sleepy town on the Brazilian Amazon. A small cadre of killers had gathered outside for a night of celebration and revelry. They had survived the war and, dammit, things weren't so bad after all. Hell, maybe it was time for a little fun.

A gaunt, unimposing male figure from perhaps a hundred yards away suddenly caught the attention of every man in the group. He was walking toward them in a manner that was troubling to them. From a distance, he seemed to be very old, with an anemic and wobbling gait, but as he approached, they could see clearly that he was relatively young, perhaps no more than thirty-five years old. What troubled them, though, was that from a distance, he appeared to be walking on the sky.

"Stay away from him. He's got the stench of the camps."

"A Jew on the grounds of Herr Himmler? Impossible!"

"You'll have to forgive me, gentlemen. It's going to take me a little while to get reacquainted with this deplorable body of mine, or what's left of it. I must say, though, you were surprisingly easy to track down. To hide in plain sight is the height of Nazi arrogance. I understand that most of your leaders have either surrendered or died by their own hand. Who's leading you now?"

"Will somebody shut him up? We can't be discussing this out here."

"He's just a starving, emaciated Jew dog. Let him talk. What does he know about anything?"

"It's 1945, isn't it. March or April, I think. I'm just guessing, though. I'm assuming you realize that eternity is only a moment. What could the Gods know of temporary existence? Eternity split into millions of little pieces?

"I can tell you that you're all about to experience that one defining moment when your angel of truth zaps your fragile little psyches with his ethereal cattle prod. My moment happened to be manifested in a singular vow of revenge. Karma, I guess you call it. Some of you may remember that I promised to give it a little nudge. And so I shall, gentlemen. So I shall."

"He's crazy! Stay away from the Jew bastard!"

"I doubt that you can still refer to me as a Jew. All that should matter to you now is my humanity, or lack thereof. And now that we have the introductions out of the way, gentlemen, would you be so kind as to remove your clothing. You're all going to be taking a little shower."

"A shower? What the hell…?"

"It's the poet! I knew I recognized him! He was crazy when they brought him in. We let him live for a few days just for laughs. He was always spouting incoherent prophesies of some sort."

"Yeah, I remember now. He called on his Jew God to bring the whole place down. He kept shouting his undying love to his wife as she was led off to the showers."

"What a jerk."

"Why didn't somebody just kill him? It doesn't make sense. A quick bullet and it's over."

"He was such a buffoon that we were all intrigued. Nobody wanted to pop him. Just let him babble. It was funny."

"You're right, gentlemen. You were all there when my wife and my thirteen-year-old daughter were led off to the showers. It was right after we entered the camp. You were all standing nearby, many of you poking and prodding. You see, gentlemen, I've done my homework. What's so frightening about a shower, they were told. We need to get rid of the lice. Now it's my turn to get rid of lice. I'll ask you again, gentlemen. Remove your clothing."

"This is insanity. Where is Herr Himmler?"

"Heinrich Himmler is dead."

"Then who invited us here?"

"I did."

"Then who the hell invited you?"

"You did, gentlemen. You all did. I should point out that the showers can be relatively quick and painless. You'll simply stop breathing. Of course, you'll attempt to breathe, but it won't be possible. What I have in mind as an option will be much more unpleasant. You see, I have some medical experiments in mind, many of them pioneered by your own Dr. Mengele.

"You can go through the relatively painless experience of gasping for your last breath, or you can choose to be sewn together by your armpits. I can assure you that you'll experience an exceedingly painful death as the inevitable infection sets in. The choice is entirely yours, gentlemen, but I'll need your immediate answer. And regardless of your decision, I'll have your clothing."

"This Jew is a raving lunatic! He has no power to do anything. Look at him. He's just a rotting Jew corpse."

"Eternity is the substance of your degradation, gentlemen; the final resolution to all your grand schemes, the final answer to your great inquisitions. It all comes down to this."

At that moment, each of the twenty-four killers realized that he was naked and utterly without recourse in a sea of chained, terrified prisoners parading through a mass of decaying bodies. The men began to panic as the hissing of the showers released a toxin into the air. A few of them began to turn blue and gasp for air, but air was always just a millimeter beyond their grasp.

Others began to mutate into monstrosities, as their fingers and eye sockets merged with the elbows and kneecaps of their fellow victims. Skin would seem to have been sewn tightly together with a simple needle and thread. The instinct for the mutants was to try to hold on to life by destroying those who were bound to them.

As the terror rose to a fever pitch, a faint and frail apparition of an angel slowly arose from the skeletal graveyard, while the imperious commands of the Russian liberators echoed throughout the camp. Auschwitz was to be no more than a memory, but for these twenty-four men, Auschwitz was to be forever.

The angelic apparition began to move among the crushed bodies of the ghosts of Auschwitz. A wraith in white, searching intently for the one she held most dear. Within moments, she emerged with the spirit of her young daughter clutched tightly around her neck. With tenderness beyond words, she caressed the spirit of her beautiful young daughter.

"You've been sleeping, my love, for death is nothing more than a dream. Life is awakening from the shadows of perpetual sleep. Continue your sleep until you're called, my darling. In time you'll awaken to the joy of meeting your beloved and starting your own family; for it was written in the stars long before you were born. You'll rise again, my darling. Until then sleep well, my sweet daughter."

After depositing the spirit of her daughter back into the skeletal pit, the angelic apparition continued to comb the spirits for a sign of her husband. After a while she found him lying in a crushed mass of sinew and broken bones. With infinite tenderness, she kneeled down and placed her bloodless lips next to his ear.

"Is this blood that consumes you, my beloved? Our love was ordained by a spirit much greater than your need for revenge. Why do you continue to fight for justice? Our bodies were never meant to last for more than these few precious seconds on earth, and yet our love still exists. Awaken now, my beloved. Take my hand and let me guide you into eternity."

But death and life are sometimes one and the same, and eternity is the blink of an eye. Her loving husband was trapped by his own unabated despair, doomed to spend his final waking moments basking in the dust of a long-forgotten death camp.

Russian soldiers were now assembling en masse to explore this baffling decimation of humanity called Auschwitz. Several of the officers seemed overwhelmed with the horror of mutilated bodies carved into a massive pile of lost lives.

"This one's still breathing, but such strange babbling for a man at death's door."

"It sounds like some sort of religious, Jew nonsense."

"What kind of a man would cling to such thoughts when he's been reduced to a pile of rubble?"

"Ellie, my angel, the kingdom of God is within us. A world of intense beauty, where love permeates the sky. That's where we were meant to live. The sky is waiting for us, my love. I know you're already there. I can see you sometimes when you come to me.

"But why did you insist on loving me? I was a wretch of a man, a non-entity shoved into a small cubicle in the back of corporate purgatory; a man with no humor and no ambition, no future and no past. What possessed you to choose me?"

The bloodless answer came from another world: a world of infinite understanding and unlimited acceptance.

"The answer, my beloved, is that I've loved you for all the things you could never see on your own. If God chooses two people to express his perfect love, then I have no reason to exist without you. Only through your eyes can I begin to understand why I was born; and in your darkest times, if you'll just look into my eyes, you'll understand your true existence."

"But I'm coming back for them, Ellie. The ones that took you at the gate."

"You already have, my beloved. You defined your moment by your need for revenge. Mine was defined by my love for you."

"But I can't let it go, Ellie. What they did to you. It's not over. Not yet. I have to go back."

"Then hold me in your dreams, my darling, for your humanity is my salvation. Just remember that death is only the beginning. You're more alive now than ever before, though your life on earth will never be the same."

He knew, of course, from the moment her eyes first touched his soul, all those years ago, that his life would never be the same.

"Goodbye then, my love," he whispered. "If eternity is only a moment, then I'll find you somewhere on the edge of my mind. I could never exist without you, Ellie. Don't forsake me, my love."

His moment had evolved into a cold, rainy afternoon in the heart of a broken bunker in Berlin. His two companions assumed he was a mirage, as no one had entered their sacred space. And yet there he was: a shivering, pathetic semblance of humanity.

A bewildered young woman with haughty eyes and an overbearing manner proceeded to castigate her uninvited guest.

"We need to be alone. This is our moment of love. Our eternity. He looks like a ghost, my husband. Has a Jew inserted itself into our wedding chamber?

"You cheap little swine," she continued. "There's absolutely no protocol that allows for this intrusion. I'll kill you myself. Have you no shame? Your demeanor and your failure to follow our dress code should be unacceptable to even the lowest levels of your hierarchy."

"Leave him alone, Eva. He's not here for you."

The gentleman with the beady eyes and small mustache turned to his uninvited guest.

"How did you know where to find me?"

"I did my homework."

"What do you intend to do to me? I have only a short time left with my bride."

"I'm not here to hurt you. I'm here simply to ask you a question."

"And what might that be?"

"How does a man keep his dignity when he's forced to exist in a cattle car for hours on end? After which, at the end of his ride, he watches his wife and daughter being raped and mutilated while he stands naked and powerless."

"You're talking from the viewpoint of a Jew. You Jews by definition are less than human. To me you're all cattle. You have no rights and you have no sense of human dignity. You might have been able to survive at the lowest level of humanity, but your greed was your undoing. Your bankers raped and mutilated our country for centuries while we stood by and did nothing. That is, until I came along. I've created power that you could never even dream of."

"But the decimation of an entire race? We watched your ascension of power. We knew this was coming, but we refused to believe it. Even now I see traces of humanity. Your kindness to your wife. The courtesies to your staff. How can this level of depravity exist within another human being?"

"What difference does it make anymore? The Third Reich has been destroyed by treachery from within. The glory of the Aryan nation will no longer exist. Jews still walk the earth."

"I don't walk, Herr Fuhrer. I fly."

With that, this most unconventional angel of death appeared to hover above the two lovers. An apparition with a sharp steel blade in two spindly arms raised high above its pathetic countenance.

The bride, in her terror, reached up and pulled a bloodless foot from the abyss. The spectral body followed in a placid, feathery plunge to the floor. The bride picked up the invisible knife and began to slash at the diaphanous foot.

There was no escape and no determination to escape, for the will of the apparition was weak and transparent. Its humble prayer was the hope of all humanity who have been crushed by forces they had no defense against.

"My God, the God of my father and mother, enrich my soul. Don't let me hurt anyone. Fill me with love, for what am I without the grace and dignity of true humanity? Take me to a better place, where all of your creation breathes the light of your infinite wisdom and compassion. Help me to end this. Somehow. Somewhere."

His moment had now progressed to a field of light rain and fleeting sunshine. Nothing of substance could be seen but the faint outline of a figure in the distance. A feeling of peace came over him for perhaps the first time in his pitiful existence, for the awareness of one's hopelessness is often one's true salvation.

Clouds punctuated the vast, unlimited horizon. The figure in the distance seemed to be beckoning him, with one hand outstretched. Was he willing, finally, to cross over the barren landscape, quiet now except for the soft shimmer of faded grass blowing in the breeze?

For the first time he understood that he was more than just the sum of his unfortunate life. The light breeze filled his lungs with a vision of unlimited love. The figure in the distance was his creator, revealed to him through the lives of those he held most dear.

"I have nothing to give," he whispered, "nothing to take. Thank you for never abandoning me. I'm ready now."

At that moment, the soul of God's creation began to fly, higher and higher into the light of God's hand, across the silent threshold of human existence, through the rain and the wind and the snow and the sun; for death, like life, is a journey, a never-ending quest for beauty, a longing that can never be filled. For what is consonance without dissonance, or release without restraint?

Somewhere in the depth of each soul lies the truth, the Holy Grail of our existence; and the truth is love; simply, unabashedly.

Late in the fall of 1945, one of the survivors of Auschwitz was able to give an account of the man the guards called "The Poet." According to the survivor, this man kept repeating "I love you," over and over, through what appeared to be every waking moment. He held on to this love of his though he was beaten and taunted to the point of unspeakable torture.

"I learned from another inmate that this poor, pathetic soul had been a bank manager in the same town where I lived. Apparently, he had a son who died of a fever at the age of nine or ten. His daughter was a little older and from all accounts was the apple of his eye. But this bank manager became a laughingstock within his organization when one of his employees accidentally discovered a stack of love letters in his desk drawer when she was looking for a document.

"It seems that nobody within the organization liked this particular bank manager, as he was severe and somewhat intolerant with everybody he came into contact with. The love letters were surreptitiously copied and passed around the office. But after a while, the laughter and derision evolved into a stunned silence as the beauty and poignancy and sheer poetry of the letters began to sink in.

"These love letters, it seems, were to his wife. What a strange concept for all who read the letters: to be that much in love with someone so familiar. The plain and simple everyday life that we all experience could actually turn out to be something so glorious, so utterly Godlike and mysterious. Why are we here? Perhaps this crazy poet was the only one who really understood the secret of our existence.

"I myself have never experienced anything quite like this love that was so obsessive to our fellow inmate. But here's the thing: this bank manager's wife actually worked for the Nazis. She wasn't even Jewish. She just fell in love with the wrong man.

"What a pity. She didn't have to be tortured like that. She was just a lowly bookkeeper in a downstairs office of the Third Reich. Nobody in the party seemed to know that she was married to a Jew until right up until the time they were herded off to Auschwitz. They say she held her daughter's hand as she was led off to the showers, but she never said a word. I guess she knew it was her time.

"Now for the really strange part of this story. Several months after the liberation of Auschwitz, I happened to walk by the same bank building where this gentleman worked. This is still my hometown, though it's truly been shattered. The bank building was closed up tight for quite a while. Too many of us taken, I guess. But we're slowly getting back to normal.

"So, I'm walking by this bank, and a piece of paper blows under my shoe. I bend over to pick it up and I notice it's got something handwritten all over it. It was badly water stained, but it seemed to be actually glowing. I know it seems improbable, but I'm thinking it's got to be from this same bank manager. Here, let me read it to you. You tell me what you think."

"God has forgiven us, my darling, for all those we've hurt in our lives; for all those we'll hurt before this is over. All that matters is the miracle of love. What other reason could there be for the splendor of fresh cut grass, or the swath of sky that I've worshiped since I was a little boy.

"You and I were here for just a few moments, but God is forever. Maybe, in some strange way, he'll decide to keep us together even now. I pledge you my belief, my darling. That's all that I have. All that I'll ever have.

"Don't forget me, my beautiful angel. I'll find you somewhere in eternity. I promise."

THE END

Las Vegas

Scorpions, rattlesnakes, and these glittering facades: the temples of hell, where the scions of superficiality stand at sentinel. Degradation made palatable by soap and sunshine; anything goes but the truth. Your only reward is the blessing of anonymity.

Las Vegas beckons you. I know … I was sucked in here too. You see, many years ago I sold my soul to the devil. I was naïve back then. They used to laugh at me and call me an "airhead." But I had something they all wanted desperately. I had the most important thing of all: I had my youth.

My boyfriend was a professor at the University. He said that I bought into the prevailing ethos that youth is life itself. He was such a sad man. He knew a lot of things, but he drank too much. I don't think he had very good self-esteem. Years later, I looked up "ethos" in a dictionary. I'm still not sure what it means.

Life was so cheap back then. I presented my body as a token to each passing glance. Once, I almost got myself killed. I presented my body to a banker from the Midwest, and he beat it to a pulp. Every bone in my face was broken.

That was the day I turned my back on youth. Now I had another reason to live. I dreamed of repaying the favor to this kindly gentleman from a small town somewhere in Nebraska (I had remembered that much). After a while I remembered everything; and then I went looking for him.

I stood on his front porch for a long time. I wanted to enjoy the moment. I was fascinated by the white picket fence that surrounded his front yard. And the rose trees! So many colors, such beauty!

I thought of his wife. I wish I hadn't thought of his wife, but I did. She had everything she could ever want, including a loving husband who doted on her every whim. He could never hurt the one he loved. He got his kicks beating up on whores.

I tried to ring the bell. I even put my finger on it, but I couldn't quite make myself do it. I was tired. All those days of living only for revenge had taken its toll. The constant pain, internal bleeding, broken ribs, a broken elbow, a broken tailbone, operations on my face. I didn't care anymore about revenge.

What would I have to gain by blowing his head off? I thought of his wife. Did I really want to do this to her? I imagined her as kind, gentle, and happy. She didn't know that she was married to a monster. But isn't there a monster inside each of us? I was so confused.

So, I did the only thing I could think of. I sat down on his front porch. What else could I do? I just sat there and waited for something to happen. And it did. He drove up. He must have been coming home from work, at that bank that I told you about.

He was dressed in his suit and tie. Boy, did he frown when he saw me sitting on his front porch, even before he got out of his car. He looked as confused as I was; and angry. I know anger when I see it, and I see it all the time.

After a few moments, he got out of his car and walked toward me.

"What can I do for you?" he said.

"Is your name really Joe Smith?" I asked.

"Yes, it is."

"I thought 'Joe Smith' is just a name people use when they have something to hide."

He shrugged. "There are a lot of Joe Smiths in this world. Now, what do you want?"

"My youth. You took it from me in a hotel room in Las Vegas. I know you don't recognize me. I was beautiful. Now, I'm not even pretty. My face is kind of distorted, don't you think?"

"For God's sake … how did you find me? I'm not going to do anything like that again. I'm sorry, just leave me alone. Please just go away, I have a family."

"If I could just believe that you're truly sorry …"

The look in his eyes was cold, unfeeling.

"What do you want from me? I'll give you money. You can give it to them. I'll give them enough to make this all worth their while. Go ahead, name a figure. But don't ever come back here and bother me or my family again. If I ever see you again, I promise you I'll turn you into dog meat, you fuckin' whore."

"Let me ask you something. Do you love your wife?"

"Of course I love my wife, you fuckin' bitch."

"Then why don't you love me?"

"What the hell is that supposed to mean?"

"I could be a wife too. I have feelings. I'm a person. I could love and be loved just like you."

I felt myself starting to shake. I thought I was going to cry, but I didn't want to cry in front of this man. And yet I couldn't help it. The tears just gushed out. It's funny, but I don't think I ever cried before.

I was a whore. I tried to make people happy. I didn't hurt anyone. I cheated a few men out of their money, I know that, but that's what I was told to do. Besides, they were drunk. They would have lost it at the tables anyway; and now they had taken my youth.

"Why did you take my youth?" I said, "it's all that I had."

The banker was sweating profusely now. I could see that his shirt was soaked. It was kind of warm outside, a little like Las Vegas; but I never saw a white picket fence in Las Vegas. He was talking on his cell phone, gesturing and kind of yelling into the phone. He was talking to somebody about me, I think.

I just wanted to leave. I just wanted to walk somewhere. So, I did. I got up from the porch and started walking down the street, past other homes with white picket fences. I wanted to find a hotel. I needed to undress in front of a man. I was a whore; I needed to be a whore again.

I walked quickly now. I saw a building. It didn't look like a hotel, but it was tall. I went inside, but I couldn't find the casino. I spotted the elevator. I stepped in and pushed the top button, number twenty-four. I got out and stepped into what must have been an office. Big floor-to-ceiling windows. So many people in their suits and ties. I ran up to one of the big windows and pressed my face and hands and body against it.

"Oh Thou," I said, "am I yours? Do I exist? Am I worthy to be loved?"

A man in a suit asked me if I was all right.

"I could love too," I said. "I know I could."

I turned to look at him. "I'm a whore," I said, "but I could be your wife."

The poor man looked shocked. He stumbled backward and tripped over a chair. I ran over to the chair, picked it up and, with all my strength, heaved it through one of the big plate glass windows.

I believe everybody in that office just stopped breathing. Nobody said a word; we all just stared at the hole in the wall. My boyfriend once told me that the only freedom we could ever have is the freedom to say no. This was my chance.

It seemed like a whole minute went by and nobody moved. Then I ran as fast as I could and, with my arms open wide, leaped through the opening headfirst. I fully expected to fly, but somebody reached out and caught my foot.

"For God's sake, help me!" he screamed. "Somebody help me!"

It hurt when he grabbed me. I couldn't tell which way was up. I was confused.

"Let go of my foot," I begged. "I've had my youth. I had a beginning; my boyfriend told me so. Now, I need to have an end. This isn't the time for your end, sir. Please let go of my foot."

Then something horrible happened. A group of men yanked and pulled on me until they got me inside, and then they pushed me up against a wall. I got real quiet because I didn't know what to do. These men looked serious, like the men who pay to be with me. They were dressed in coats and ties, but they didn't look like office workers.

After a minute, they started tugging at me and pulling me away from the wall until they had me surrounded. I turned my head from side to side, looking into each man's eyes, trying to find a spark of emotion.

Then one man stepped forward. He wasn't calm like the others. He was in his shirtsleeves, and it looked like he had been running, He was sweating, and appeared to be very agitated.

"I'm sorry I was late getting here," he said to the others. "I just missed her plane. I had to wait at the airport for over an hour to get the next flight out."

Then he yelled at the office workers.

"I want everybody who works here to leave the room immediately. You're through for the day. It's been cleared with your superiors. The window will be fixed before you come back to work tomorrow. Now everybody take what you need and leave the room quietly and promptly. Do it now."

Papers started shuffling as the office workers prepared to leave the room. It was strange, but the man in shirtsleeves never took his eyes off mine, even while he was shouting at the office workers. They were cold, those eyes … cold and cruel. I knew those eyes. I had felt them watching me before, while I was with other men.

After the office workers left, it got real quiet. I think it was some kind of a standoff. The men encircling me just stared at me. No one said a word. I turned my head quickly from side to side, looking into each man's eyes, trying to find something to latch onto. I had no frame of reference. I simply didn't know what to do.

Finally, the silence was broken. The leader, the man in shirtsleeves, said, "Why are you here, Lisa?"

Lisa! He knew my name!

"Why are you here, Lisa? Tell us. We'd like to know."

His voice was almost gentle.

"I wanted revenge," I said, "but then I didn't want revenge. I just wanted to find love. I could love too, you know. I could be a wife if only somebody would marry me. I could have roses and a white picket fence; and I could love, with all my heart and soul."

The men all started laughing … kind of a nervous laugh. I didn't know that I was being funny, but sometimes I get confused. I had made them laugh.

One of the men said, "For Christ's sake, she thinks she has a soul."

That struck the rest of them as funny, and they all started laughing again, except for the leader, the man in shirtsleeves. He smiled a little, though, and said, "Lisa, we all know that you have a great capacity for love. Nobody loves like Lisa … longer and harder than all the rest of the whores in Las Vegas put together. Isn't that right, gentlemen?"

The men all whooped and hollered and laughed and patted each other on the back; and then I realized that I knew these men … professionally. Each of them had been my customer many times, but I couldn't remember anything more about them. It was like a dream.

"Gentlemen," he continued, "it appears that Lisa has been looking for love. In fact, she came all this way to find one of our clients who gave her a lot of love on his last trip to Las Vegas. She scared him to death about an hour ago. She hunted him down. If his wife had been home, it might have cost him his marriage. He's not very happy with us right now, Lisa. In fact, we've lost him as a valuable client … at about a million dollars a year."

"I wanted revenge," I said, "but then I didn't want revenge. I just wanted to find love."

"All right, Lisa, I'm going to grant you your wish. You're going to find the love you've been searching for. In fact, I'm not even sure that you're up to it, and you're the best, baby."

He started to take off his clothes. "Don't mind me, Lisa. I'm just going to watch. You see, Lisa, I'm a scientist; but, when it comes right down to it, these guys are just a bunch of good ol' boys dressed up in monkey suits."

The men started whooping and hollering again.

"Boys, Lisa wants to find some love. If you value your jobs and your careers, you're going to goddamn well give it to her. I want this to be the gangbang of the century; Lisa's final performance. Do you understand what I'm saying, boys? I want you to go after the little bitch; but, first, let me get my camera."

He ran over to a bag that had been placed on a chair and pulled out a video camera. He looked very excited. Some of the men started taking off their clothes. When they do that, I'm supposed to take off my clothes, so I undressed completely.

All of a sudden, I felt a sharp pain in the back of my left leg, behind my kneecap. Somebody had whacked me really hard with something that felt like metal. I turned my head quickly to look at the place where they hit me. I didn't see any blood, but my leg looked bruised and twisted. One of the men was holding a metal pipe.

The men were laughing so hard that it gave me a few seconds to test my leg. It hurt like hell. I was holding it up off the ground because it hurt so much. I didn't know what to do, so I started hopping around in a circle on my good leg. That made the men really laugh.

Then the men all jumped on me and started gangbanging me. I knew what it was because my owners had described it to me. They said they would never let it happen to me if I did my job and worked hard. But it *was* happening to me. They were all yelling and screaming and laughing and doing it to me from behind and in the mouth and … you know … all sorts of ways, while others were beating me with their fists.

It hurt so bad that I wished I could die, but I didn't know how to die. I just kept looking from face to face, trying to find a trace of humanity; but there wasn't any humanity. Maybe they weren't human anymore.

I tried so hard not to pass out. My owners got mad if I passed out when men were doing it to me, because they'd have to give some of the money back. The men who beat me wanted me to stay awake, so they could see me in terrible pain. That's what they paid for.

While they were gangbanging me, another man ran into the room and started shouting at the others. I recognized his voice. It was my boyfriend! He made the men stop beating me. He yelled at them. Their leader, the man with the camera, yelled back at him. They yelled and yelled at each other. Finally, the men put on their clothes and left. My boyfriend stayed with me.

"I'm sorry they got here before I did, Lisa," he said. "I'm so sorry."

"Am I going to die?" I knew that I was closer to death than I had ever been.

He kneeled over me and held my hand. I looked up into his sad, kind face. I felt that my heart would burst out of my body, I was so happy. Nobody had ever held my hand before.

"You're not going to die, Lisa. Let yourself pass out. It's O.K. You're in more pain than you can possibly stand. There are more men coming, good men, who will help me keep you alive. So, pass out; give into it. No one will be mad at you."

I must have started to pass out, because I was in terrible pain; but then another man, an attorney for some corporation, came into the room. My boyfriend thought I had passed out, but I could hear them talking.

"All right, what the hell's going on?" said the attorney. "Who is she? And why do we have the most prominent banker in this hick town threatening to sue us for a hundred million dollars? Something about us exposing him as some kind of a monster. He said we signed an agreement of confidentiality. What is he talking about? If we did, it sure as hell didn't come through my department.

"Who is she? And what the hell is wrong with her? Good God, look at her! She's been beaten half to death.

Have you called an ambulance? You can see that she's in terrible pain. What happened to her?"

"Nothing happened to her that's not supposed to happen to her."

"She's supposed to be beaten like this?"

My boyfriend didn't say anything. I don't think he wanted to talk about it.

"What's going on here, you bastard? You know I'm not going to take any of your shit."

My boyfriend let out a long sigh and then walked over to a couch and sat down.

"She's a Pleasure Machine. We manufacture them in Las Vegas. Any fetish you could possibly want, she'll accommodate you. If you want to beat the shit out of her, that's all right; we can put her back together again. That doesn't make this guy a monster. He was told that he could beat her to a pulp. He paid for it!"

"I can't believe you were able to keep this from me."

"We kept it from a lot of people."

"So, it was strictly contained on a local level?"

"We realized it would never work outside of Las Vegas. People accept things there."

"Then what's this one doing twelve hundred miles from Las Vegas?"

"I don't know all the details yet, but I'm sure it's going to be one hell of a story."

"But she feels pain. Look at her, she feels pain."

"I know she does. We had to program the capacity for pain to make it realistic. Nobody would pay to beat up a piece of tin. We had to program humanity, for Christ's sake, or it wouldn't work."

"Humanity? How in the hell do you program humanity? Only God can program humanity."

"We had to simulate humanity. We didn't try to play God. We just had to get it close enough that people would pay the big bucks. We're entrepreneurs after all; we're not scientists."

"My God, what have you done? Look at her. She's in agony. You didn't create a Pleasure Machine. You created someone to torture. Someone with feelings. Someone who wants to live and be loved, to be normal. But you created her to be tortured over and over with no hope of escape; no means of escape. How did you simulate humanity?"

My boyfriend leaned over and held his head.

"Do we really need to get into this?"

"How did you simulate humanity, damn you. Tell me!"

"We tried to add what we thought was the essence of love."

"The essence of love? Jesus! How do you even define the essence of love?"

"It wasn't that hard to figure out. Look around you. The essence of love is the need to care for others more than you care for yourself. She's loaded with it. We laid it on thick. That's the only way she could handle all this punishment."

"Holy Christ! What a bunch of callous bastards. Can't you give her something for the pain?"

"She's O.K. for now. I told her to pass out. Our doctors will be here any minute."

"Who were the goons I passed on the way up?"

"They're all security from Las Vegas. The chief of security refers to himself as a 'scientist.' He's actually a degenerate, faggot son-of-a-bitch who likes to watch. If he knew I was telling you this he'd probably have me killed.

"The only reason I was able to get rid of the bastard is that I still outrank him. I was lucky. When I saw the mood they were in, I thought they were going to kill me and report it as an accident."

"All right, I'll go try to calm the banker down … offer him some big bucks. Maybe we can throw in another trip to Las Vegas. Get him back on track."

"It can all be arranged."

The attorney shook his head. "You've come a long way, haven't you, Gary. To think I was the one who brought you into the company. The philosopher, we used to call you in school. The agnostic. The guy with his head in the clouds. Always way out there. So now you program humanity. Well, I hope you're proud of your work."

"More than you know."

"All right, let me get on this. I'll get back to you in a couple of hours."

He started to leave. "Oh, by the way, the banker complained that she was praying in his driveway."

"Praying?"

"That's what I said, you prick … praying. I guess that's one thing she couldn't have learned from you. She also threatened to blow his head off."

"Christ, no wonder the guy's in a panic. Look inside her purse and see if she has a gun."

The attorney fumbled through my purse. "No sign of a gun."

"I guess I'm not surprised," said my boyfriend. "She must have learned the concept of revenge through watching television in the hotel rooms. She just never learned that to 'blow someone's head off' you would need a gun."

"She's got a wallet in here with several hundred dollars and a phony driver's license."

"We told her to keep the ID with her at all times. She has to show it sometimes to get past hotel security."

"Look at this. She taped the word 'money' in big letters onto the side of her wallet. How childlike."

"She was created in a laboratory three years ago. Of course she's childlike. She hovers on the fringes of reason, of judgment. She wants to go forward, but it's hard for her to assimilate blocks of experience. We have to feed her small pieces of information at a time, and even then she struggles to understand.

"You have to realize that she was created to live out her whole existence in hotel rooms. We'll let her watch a little television in the hotel rooms; but when she was recuperating from that last beating they sometimes forgot about her, and she'd watch it all day long.

"That's dangerous. It's important that we monitor every piece of information that goes into her brain. This little trip proves that she's had too much time alone. What else is in the purse?"

"A page from a book."

"What book? Where did she get hold of a book? We don't let her read books, only magazines."

That's when I knew I had to answer him. I was in pain, but I was able to sit up a little bit. I just had to tell him.

"I'll tell you," I said, "but it's a secret."

My boyfriend looked startled. He was surprised that I was awake.

"Lisa, we've been wondering about your book. Where did you get it?"

"It's a secret," I said, "but I have to tell you. One night a man stuck my head in a drawer next to the bed. Then he pushed on the drawer really hard, trying to crush my head. It worked. He really hurt me. My teeth were smeared into my cheekbone.

"He slammed my head in the drawer over and over. Then he went into the bathroom. I could hear him throwing up. I almost passed out from the pain, but I could see something in the drawer with me. Everything was in a haze, but I could see it clearly. It was a book; but it was more than a book. It was love."

"Of course, Lisa, of course. You were bound to stumble on to it sooner or later. It's a standard part of the security checklist to have it removed from any hotel room where you meet with your clients; but somebody must have been careless that night."

"Why didn't you tell me about love?"

"I don't know, Lisa. Perhaps I felt it was outside of my area of expertise. I was brought in to impart culture, refinement, a sense of philosophy, a sense of balance. You were to be everything that a man could desire. My job, I suppose, was to transform you into a woman of superior breeding.

"Lisa, I imparted so much wisdom to you, yet all of my cynicism didn't make a dent. You're as naïve and decent and pure as if you had never known me, as if men had never touched you. The syndicate has brutalized you for three solid years, Lisa. They've made so much money off your pain. You've made them a fortune.

"You were the first, Lisa, the prototype. They watched your every move. You were monitored around the clock, but something went wrong. You had the need to think for yourself. You wanted to grow. You wanted to understand the humanity that was placed inside of you. That was never their intention, Lisa. They knew this could be a problem.

"So, they reasoned with you. They tried to beat it out of you. But nothing could stop you from wanting to think for yourself. The ones that followed you behaved perfectly, but they weren't as popular with the customers. They were like voluptuous blow-up dolls; willing to do anything, never complaining.

"But you had a mind of your own. Sometimes you even talked back to the customers. Maybe that's why they all asked for you. They said you really got them riled up. When they whacked you it really hurt, didn't it, Lisa."

"Yes."

"Men like that, Lisa. They receive tremendous satisfaction from cracking your skull open and watching you writhe on the ground in horrific pain. This doesn't mean anything to you, Lisa, but men have paid up to a quarter of a million dollars for one appointment with you. We can't even get fifty thousand for the others. Hell, some of them we can't even give away. They don't seem to be real. But you, Lisa … in some ways you're almost human."

"I am human."

"Lisa, you're a machine."

"But I could love. I know I could."

"Lisa, we put that inside of you. We programmed that into you, but it only goes so far."

"You programmed me, but you didn't create me."

"Who created you, Lisa?"

"Thou."

"Thou? What do you mean by 'Thou,' Lisa?"

The attorney jumped in. "It's all over the page from her purse. The damn thing is covered in blood. She must have been in a hell of a lot of pain when she wrote it. The pen strokes are broken and distorted, but that's what it is. It's the word 'Thou,' scribbled all over the page; and it looks like she tried to circle something on the page."

"What did you circle, Lisa?"

"When I walk through the valley of death I will fear no evil; for Thou is with me."

"You're in way over your head, Lisa. I'm going to have to insist that you lie down now and be quiet until the doctors get here."

"I don't want them touching me anymore."

"Why not, Lisa?"

"Because I'm not just a body."

I wanted so much to get up from the floor. Oh, if I only had the strength, I thought. I pushed and pushed until a hand lifted me up. It was Thou. I started hopping on my good leg over to the hole in the wall. There was a small ledge outside. I hung on to the broken glass on the window and hopped onto the ledge. I could see all the way down to the street.

My boyfriend jumped up from the couch and hurried toward me.

"Lisa, get away from there. You're going to fall."

"Oh Thou," I prayed, "into thy hands I commend my spirit."

"Lisa, for God's sake, you still have time. They're not through with you yet. Sure, they're mad that you took off on your own and hounded an important client. They were very, very upset with you, Lisa; but all will be forgiven. They'll just tighten the clamps a little bit. You've made them rich, and they're greedy bastards. They're not about to jeopardize their incredible flow of income.

"I was sent here to bring you back so the others wouldn't beat you to death. They were afraid those lunatics would mangle you beyond repair. But I saved you, Lisa. They want you back. You'll have time to watch TV, and even read if you'd like."

I kept looking down at the street. I could see people on the sidewalk. They were free.

"I'm going to fly."

"Lisa, please don't do this to me. The last thing the syndicate needs is publicity."

"Let her go," said a voice from the entrance. "Let's see if she can fly. Hell, she can do everything else." It was the scientist. He had a gun.

My boyfriend whirled around toward the entrance. "I thought I told you to stay away from here. The syndicate wants her back in one piece. Now, get out of here and let me do my job."

"You don't have a job anymore, Gary. I'm taking over."

"Sam, haven't you screwed things up enough? Just let me take care of this. She always does what I tell her to do."

The scientist smiled. "Gee, really? I guess that means you've been getting a lot of blow jobs."

"Look, this is between you two," said the attorney, as he bolted toward the door. "I've got an appointment."

"One more step and I'll take off your kneecap," said the scientist. He was aiming his gun right at the attorney's knees.

The attorney stopped abruptly. He looked really nervous.

"What are you doing? I don't have anything to do with this. I'm just trying to help out. I'm not going to be a problem for you."

"Damned right, you're not. Now get down on your knees."

"What? For Christ's sake, man, I'm not the enemy. We both work for the same corporation. I'm not here to cause you any problems."

"It's going to be a lot easier to get down on your knees while you still have knees."

"Leave him alone, Sam," said my boyfriend. "He's here because the syndicate believes he's the only one who can straighten out this mess you got us into. He's not here to hurt you. He's here to help."

"Get down on your fuckin' knees, you corporate son-of-a-bitch."

"All right, all right," said the attorney.

He looked scared to death as he dropped down to his knees.

"You're next, Gary. Get on your knees."

"Sam, don't do this. We're all on the same team."

"I never liked you, Gary. You mean nothing to me. Now get on your knees."

My boyfriend slowly dropped to his knees.

"Sam, think about what you're doing. This isn't the way to …"

"Hey Gary, look at this one," laughed the scientist. He was staring at the attorney. The attorney had started to cry.

"What's the problem, you wimpy motherfucker?"

"Please, I've got a wife," the attorney begged.

"Really?" said the scientist. "You'll have to tell me the cunt's name. I'll give her a call. Let her know you went down like a man."

He cocked the trigger and shot the attorney right through the chest.

"For God's sake!" yelled my boyfriend. "Sam, don't do this. I don't want to die. I've got so much work left to do. Please, Sam, don't kill me."

"Fuck you, Gary," said the scientist. Then he shot my boyfriend through the heart.

"No! No!" I cried. "Not my boyfriend. No! No! No! You killed my boyfriend."

The scientist laughed. He was having fun.

"Come down from your perch, little Lisa. Where are you going? One step backward and you'll fall twenty-four stories. That's a long way, Lisa." He started walking toward me.

"Will I die?"

"They won't let you die, Lisa, even if they have to scrape you off the sidewalk with a spatula. Your wonderful, beautiful life will go on and on," he laughed. "You make way too much money for them, Lisa.

"I'm the one who's going to die. When you took your little trip, that was the end of it for me. For you to get out in the open like that was unforgivable. I was careless, Lisa. I didn't think you had it in you.

"But you're a clever girl, aren't you. You actually think for yourself. Can you imagine that? A machine gets to make decisions that affect people's lives. You're deciding right now whether or not to jump, aren't you. I say, don't do it. It doesn't make any sense to jump if you can't die. Why don't you come back inside and we'll talk about it"

He put his hand out. I turned my head and looked behind me, all the way down to the street. I kind of wanted to go there; but, before I could decide what to do, he yanked me by the arm and pulled me inside. I tumbled over a chair and hit the floor really hard.

He started laughing and kicking me, so I started to crawl. I didn't know what else to do. I crawled over to the attorney, and then I crawled right over his chest. I could hear his heart beating. He was still alive.

Then I crawled over to my boyfriend. He was dead. I was so sad for him. He didn't want to die. I curled up and lay my head on his chest. The monster kept kicking me, harder and harder; but then he stopped and tossed his gun on the floor, next to my boyfriend.

"I'm going to have me a quickie," he announced. That surprised me, because I thought he only liked to watch. I turned over on my back, with my head still on my boyfriend's chest.

"But you're a scientist," I said.

He laughed. "In the interest of science, I want to see if I can do it."

Then he dropped his pants and climbed on top of me. He was really rough with me. He penetrated me, but in the wrong place. It was over in a few seconds, but it seemed to give him even more energy. He acted like he was delirious.

"God, you're a great fuck!" he screamed.

He was so worked up that he found the strength to do pushups while still penetrating me. Faster and faster, he pushed with his arms. Up and down forty times, fifty times, a hundred times.

Finally, he collapsed on top of me; his hot breath burning into my shoulder. He panted heavily for a few minutes, but then he got real quiet, as if he had stopped breathing. He seemed to be listening for something. He must have heard the click.

We both waited and waited until, finally, he couldn't take it anymore. He got real nervous and his body started to shake. The pressure must have got to him. I think he needed to look me in the eyes. He raised his head very slowly until our eyes were only inches apart.

"To blow someone's head off," I said, "you would need a gun."

His eyes got real big, and he tried to put his hand up to cover his face. I missed and shot him in the neck. He looked surprised. He put his hand over the hole in his neck and started to choke and gasp for air. I tried again. This time I blew his head off. His brain spurted out sideways.

I blew the smoke off the barrel of the gun like they do on TV, but then I realized I didn't have a holster, so I just kept the gun in my hand. I tried to push him off me, but he wouldn't budge. I pushed and pushed and pushed. I didn't know what else to do, so I just lay there for a while and tried to think.

The pain had started to get real bad, and I wasn't sure how long I could take it. Maybe, just this one time, I should let myself pass out. Maybe, just this once, it would be all right. I woke up three months later.

I'm almost human, so I have to go through a natural recuperation process. My owners decided that I should sleep while my body was healing because I had gone through so much stress. I woke up confused; then something terrible happened. My spirit died and I got old. I looked the same, of course, but something was different. Men stopped asking for me.

My owners told me to "act" young or they'd have me destroyed, but I could never understand what "act" means. So, they decided to destroy me and maybe keep some of the parts for emergencies. But one man insisted they could still salvage me, that I could still be of use to the syndicate.

I went to work as a maid. The man from the syndicate said that I had made a very difficult kill, and that I could be invaluable as an assassin. Over the next five years, I killed forty-seven men. Not one of them suspected the maid. Some of them even tried to make a pass at me.

My owners told me I could sleep with the men before I killed them. I was too old to be a whore, but some of the men liked the idea of sleeping with their maid.

I'm eight years old now. My owners told me to stop thinking about love. They said that I look like I'm twenty, but I act like I'm fifty. They said that nobody would love a fifty-year-old whore. I told them I'm not a whore; I'm a maid. That started them laughing. They laughed so hard they had tears in their eyes. One of them said, "You're the best, baby."

Well, I'd better get some sleep. I start work at seven in the morning. I'm a maid, and I've got an important kill tomorrow. He's staying at a hotel on the Strip. I'll kill him and then I'll put a "do not disturb" sign on his door.

Sometimes they let me hold the gun that I'll use for the next day's kill. They want to see what I'll do with it; it amuses them. Ouch! I just shot myself in the temple. I keep trying, but the bullet always bounces off. They took the gun away from me, and now they're laughing at me.

My owners are the "scions of superficiality." You didn't think I wrote that, did you? I found it in my boyfriend's papers after he died. I think it means that Las Vegas will always be Las Vegas.

They're laughing at me now. I never learned how to laugh. My boyfriend never taught me, and he's dead. But I guess I'm not so different from most people in Las Vegas. We can't laugh, though there's laughter all around us.

God has forgotten us, but I haven't forgotten him. His book is in the drawer next to the bed. After every kill, I read about love before I make my escape.

I think I've learned a secret. I don't want my owners to know my secret, but I'll tell you. I think somehow God and I are the same. It's in his book of love. "As you do to the least of these, so you do to me."

Will you help me? If you ever come to Las Vegas, will you look for me? I won't hurt you. I only kill bad men.

My owners added the "essence of love" when they made me. They laid it on thick. Then they tried to reason with me.

They tried to beat it out of me. Now, they think I'm the devil's child. They don't know my secret.

But you do.
Goodnight.

THE END

Elegy

Why is today so different from any other day? The colors are different. The echoes, the vibrations. Even the rain is different. Someone from another world is calling.

Catherine at twenty-six, classically beautiful and unflinchingly regal, had been working for the past two years in the editor's department of a prestigious fashion magazine in Manhattan. Late on a withering fall afternoon, during the peak of crimson colors, she caught a glimpse of someone from another world, or was it a dream, deep into a past that never was.

Her instincts were to stumble into the waiting taxi, but instead she found herself retreating to the foyer of her office building. A brutal, intense sadness had overwhelmed her senses. A previous life was calling her.

"Why are you doing this to me?" she whispered. "What could I possibly have to offer you? I have a world right here in front of me. How can I disappear into a place that doesn't exist?"

She began to wonder if her knees would collapse before she could make it to the elevator, but within a few moments, she found herself crumpled in the swivel chair behind her desk on the 33rd floor. No one else could have understood the depth of her sadness at this moment, this profound recognition of her true existence.

"How can you judge me? If I've lived a glorious life or a wretched life, what does it matter? If eternity is simply the blink of an eye, then isn't love the only thing that matters? Let me live in this world. You owe me that much. Love will find me again. It has to, or I'll simply be taking up space."

It was October of 1972. Fashion was garish and fickle, but Catherine had always been a stickler for perfection. The bead of sweat on her brow was most certainly unfashionable. She could never be enticed by the tawdry allure of mini-skirts and purple jumpsuits. She was entrenched in the fashion world as a woman of the highest manner of purifying elegance.

The next morning, she called her supervisor with news of her sudden illness, explaining that she "may have picked up something." She spent several minutes on the decision to go with 'may' over 'might.' Throughout the afternoon she remained self-quarantined in her Lilliputian apartment overlooking Central Park. She rarely moved, for she instinctively felt that the very act of walking would create a bridge from this dimension to the next.

Life is so beautiful, she thought, as she gazed into the memories of her past few months on earth. Somewhere within this fleeting semblance of humanity, my peers have begun to accept me as the consummate professional, guiding me through intensive discourse on the evolution of fashion, agreeing to respect my tentative positions, as I have theirs.

To be a part of this creative force has brought me the greatest happiness I've ever known. For isn't our true existence a constant state of reaching for the unreachable? To live, to really live, is to position our finite minds deep within the electricity that flows throughout each human soul. For the first time, perhaps, I've succeeded in allowing this energy to define who I really am.

At exactly 4:45 that afternoon, Catherine ascended from her lonely fortress and walked out into the cold, autumn wind. From the roof of her apartment building, she could see the whole of Manhattan. The breeze was bitter and foreboding, blinding in its intensity, and yet her eyes remained lucid. Her mind was clear. There could be no regret. It was her time.

At the exact moment she stepped off the roof, a ferocious gust of wind propelled her back onto the ledge. Her fingernails ripped into the bricks as the instinct for survival exploded throughout her consciousness. The tornado on the ledge was deafening in its force. A thousand freight trains passed through her mind and over her body.

Within moments, as the torrent subsided into silence, her tears began to fall. Wistfully, longingly, she remembered the question that we all must ask ourselves throughout the span of our lives: Why am I here? A grain of sand in time and scope, and yet painfully aware of the unlimited love that exists within each of us.

Far below the roof of her apartment building, chaos ensued. Waves of shock engulfed the horror-struck crowd as sirens raged in the distance. Denizens of the streets, aligned in momentary solidarity, stared in disbelief at the disheveled body of a beautiful young woman sprawled across the hood of a taxicab.

Perhaps she might have taken more time to ponder her decision to leave this world, but in reality, her body was immediately sacrificed from the ledge. For no one can live two lives at once. We must choose. She chose simply to follow her spirit, trapped somewhere in the sphere that separates life from death.

Later that evening, a nighttime custodian discovered what appeared to be an "angelic substance" on a particular chair in the editorial office on the 33rd floor of the Fashion Building, a white ooze of some sort with what seemed to be a transparent robe draped over the top of it. This was so unnerving to the custodian that he collapsed on the floor and quickly scurried under a neighboring desk.

He realized over the next few minutes that he was unable to move his limbs, as he had become petrified with fear. When he finally mustered the courage to crawl out from under the desk, he was immediately accosted by another substance, this time from a distance: a dark, foreboding image of a man standing in the doorway to the office.

The custodian was convinced at this point that he had died and gone to hell. It was the drinking, he thought. He had beaten the wife a couple of times last month. Nothing serious. Just a few bruises and maybe a dislocated elbow. Maybe she didn't deserve it. It was the damn drinking.

"Oh God," he thought. "The Devil's come to get me."

A swill of sacrilege, purveyed in Latin, foamed through the tongues of the demon. "Ego sum via, veritas, et vita. Et omnium Deorum Deus. Et erunt mihi in otio permanere ad excidium exlecebra mactasses." ("I am the way, the truth, and the life. The God of all Gods. I will continue to bludgeon and rape at my leisure.")

The immediacy of a mere human presence was ignored, for the demon had an army of millions not unlike the custodian. He was there to deal with one concern only: the fluttering of wings. With a wave of his hand, the multi-tongued demon pronounced sentence on the doomed custodian. "Iniunctione cruciatus ignis." ("Excruciation by the infliction of fire.")

A national tabloid ran a story a few days later about a beautiful young woman emerging from a building on Fifth Avenue at approximately 5:45 am. She was seen walking slowly down the street as if in a trance. A homeless man who had been sleeping on the street had approached her to ask for money, but when he got within a few feet of her, he suddenly collapsed and began begging for mercy. He said that she looked at him with compassion, but continued to walk down the street without saying a word. When she reached the end of the block, she suddenly unfolded her enormous wings and began to fly directly into the wind.

The police commissioner found that he was suddenly drawn into a fable that could never have happened. Once upon a time an angel appeared on Fifth Avenue. She was seen leaving a building shortly before sunrise. Coincidentally, a beautiful fashion designer had abruptly disappeared from the same building the previous afternoon. Could the fashion designer have transformed into an angel? And for Christ's sake, do angels really have wings?

"Let's back up and take this from the beginning. A night custodian was found deceased under a desk on the 33rd floor of the Fashion Building on Fifth Avenue. It looked like a simple heart attack except for one thing: The guy had a look of pure terror frozen on his face. The lady exiting from the building sprouted wings and flew away. Pretty convenient if you ask me.

"I realize our esteemed mayor will feel the need to weigh in on this. But if you think about it, any rumble of attention generated by an 'angel sighting' will evolve into a fate similar to those prickly UFO sightings: forgotten with a shrug, as in 'So what?' Now let me get on with my damn job."

Two years earlier, the cold winter mornings of Manhattan recalled the sad, haunted sound of a cello. The bottom note of a cello is a low C, but no piece of music could linger there for long. Those who linger on a low C would be in danger of sliding into madness.

Throughout her young adulthood, Catherine had dedicated herself to joyfully tackling a vast repertoire of cello sonatas, right up until the moment when she began her startling descent into the demon-infested playground known as Manhattan. As depression began to decimate her life, the cello became a constant reminder of a dream that had begun to slip away: her goal of becoming the principal cellist of the New York Philharmonic.

The death of her young daughter had created an impossible conflict of duty and soul, compounded by the absence of a husband who had slithered off into nothingness. Her husband was at one time an accomplished artist of some acclaim, but an overwhelming addiction to bright lights and cheap alcohol had recently devolved into a desperate and delinquent low C. He was nowhere to be seen.

Catherine's musical abilities and passion for beauty were anathema to the desires of the grotesque community of demons infiltrating the city. She was much too beautiful, dignified, and peaceful to be allowed to function undisturbed. While attempting to survive a horrendous gang rape by the sons of Baal, Catherine was seen crawling out to her beloved flower bed; a broken, withered young woman, collapsing into a fetal position, with memories so torrid as to be unfathomable.

Somewhere in the next few hours, life would begin again. They had tried to save her in the hospital. Her life was lost, but her soul would survive. An overwhelming sense of love is stronger than the forces of darkness.

The Archangel Michael was appointed to be her mentor and protector, yet he was determined to let her stumble through on her own. Angelic substance evolved into the body she knew so well, but memories would remain hidden and impossibly painful. Within a few days, she was assigned to a desk on the 33rd floor of the Fashion Building. The hiring executive demanded to know her qualifications for employment. She replied simply that she was addicted to elegance.

Over time, the world of high fashion would reveal itself in all its splendor. Clothing lines would be covered extensively, but Catherine consistently resisted ideas that were malignant to her elevated sense of ensemble and proportion. A beautiful woman would have no interest in wearing something cheap or unflattering. A woman without physical beauty would be drawn to a much more powerful world of inner beauty. Elegance, to Catherine, was never a pose or an affectation. It was a sense of uplifting the spirit.

More than anything, she wanted to love again. How many times had she dreamed of a lost love from another world? If she could only remember. But for personal matters she could barely remember yesterday. It was all a blur. Where was she born? Who were her parents?

She had no idea that the world she perceived was merely a training ground for an existence far beyond anything she had ever imagined. For what are memories but discarded hallucinations, flickering like dying stars through the haze of time?

Her metamorphosis, after her fall, was exceptionally difficult. The 33rd floor of the Fashion Building was the focal point of her awareness. She remained there in spirit for a period of time, but the demons that haunt Manhattan had taken an unusual interest in her presence. Demons rarely allow themselves to become involved in the perceived childish behavior of novice angels. The thought of watching angelic toddlers take baby steps is extremely unpleasant to the underworld.

And yet, there was something different about this one. The decision to move on to a higher calling by ending her own life was infuriating to Baal, the God of demons. Over the centuries he had watched countless people take their own lives, mostly to rid themselves of the excruciating pain inflicted by his followers. But for a novice angel, who hadn't even attained her wings, to deliberately step off of a building presumes a position of strength. Is Michael behind this? Why this one? What makes her so goddamned saintly?

"Michael! I know you can hear me! It seems that I have an affinity for Latin, but I'll make this simple for you, in pure vernacular. It's time to cut your losses and hand over that brain-dead, bleeding-heart beginner you've been protecting, the pathetic little twit who stepped off the building. She's not worthy of her wings. I'll fuse her tongue together with my tongues. We'll have a tongue fest. You can join in if you'd like!

"Michael, you poor dumb fool, you deserve better than this. All that work for a God who continually abandons you. What has he done for you lately? He forces you to mentor the weakest of the weak, and then he drops them like a lead cherub.

"Come and worship me, Michael. You can bring all your friends. Gabriel, Raphael, Uriel, all of them. I'm compassionate, Michael. I'll take care of you. Of course, I'll have to remove your wings to keep you from getting in a snit and flying away, but I'll let you walk around like normal people. Maybe even dress you in a suit and tie. What do you say, Michael?

"Don't ignore me, Michael. You know I won't have this 'holier-than-thou' bitch flitting around my kingdom. She doesn't remember this, but we've had our way with her before. She used to play the cello. Can you imagine that? An ugly bitch like that trying to conjure up the angels."

Michael answered with silence, for he was no match for Baal, neither physically nor intellectually. His only weapon was to provoke by refusing to respond, for the God of demons hated to be ignored.

At about the same time, a frazzled man in his early thirties stumbled into the waiting room of an obscure medical facility on the lower east side of Manhattan. He thought he had been bitten by a bat. His pulse was sinking rapidly. His intuition told him that he was about to die. His intuition was right, for intuition is a ladder into the soul: to stand at the entrance of eternity and know that you can never turn back.

It seems unlikely that a loser like David, who had lingered on the streets in an alcoholic haze, would ever be accepted into the glorious world of angelic intercession. He was admitted simply because he believed in something deeper and wider than his own existence. His qualifications at his death were the same as yours or mine: He had lost everything.

Early the next morning, David received his first assignment as a cadet. He was to begin working immediately as a janitor at a prominent office building on 5th avenue. He would be responsible for the upkeep of five of the upper floors, including the 29th through the 33rd floors.

His initiation came quickly. On his first night he thought he heard voices coming from under a desk in an office on the 33rd floor. The voices seemed multi-dimensional and indiscernible, as if a group of petitioners were "speaking in tongues." The flow of conversation quickly emerged from under the desk and began to move effortlessly throughout the room, imbuing the unseen congregation with a sense of authority and confidence.

David could feel his heart pounding. "Who are you talking to? I'm just the janitor."

The drone of voices became overwhelmingly intense, as if the forgotten voices of all mankind were lifting their spirits to heaven, praying for the strength to survive another day.

"What can I possibly have to offer you? I'm just a janitor."

The voices continued to ascend as David collapsed into a chair and began to vomit into a waste basket. He couldn't remember ever feeling this depth of despair.

"This overwhelming sense of love is destroying my life."

"Destroying, my ass. Try embellishing."

"I can't believe you said that. Aren't you the one who gave me this assignment? Why did you put me in this position? And why can't I see you?"

"Keep babbling like that and you never will. I'm known as Gabriel. We brought you here because we believe you're the only one who can draw out someone very important to us. We can't find her and she won't come to us."

"Then why would she come to me?"

"It's complicated. Let's just say that a lost love still haunts a piece of her mind. You ran from her once when she needed you. There's nothing more painful than the loss of a child, David. You experienced the same loss, but you abandoned the one who needed you most. She won't abandon you."

"I don't remember any of this."

"Exactly."

"But what about all those voices?"

"When archangels travel together, they're sure to attract a crowd. It's not your concern."

"But isn't that part of my assignment? To help people?"

"You have something more pressing to deal with. Someone evil has been alerted to your presence. Someone encompassing the full force of the underworld. Your responsibility now is to try to hold your position. It won't be easy, but we can only protect you if you're willing to protect yourself."

"Protect myself from …?"

"The Devil himself, brother. Just try not to pee your pants. He'll come at you with everything he has. Just remember, he's not here for you. You're just bait. Keep your cool and you'll be all right."

At that moment, Baal stood head-to-head with the hapless janitor. The God of demons was somewhat intrigued that this forgotten piece of human detritus had been allowed to soar to even the minimum level of angelic cadet.

"Tu mente stultus insipidum. You mindless, insipid fool. Would you listen to a weak, spineless parasite like Gabrielle? Jealous to his entrails that he's not first in charge, instead of his lover, Michael? But you, stench most foul, scum of the streets, how did you ever arrive at this hallowed location? You must bow down and worship Baal, your one true God, before we continue this unpleasant conversation.

"You're too scared to even move? Just drop to your knees. Are you stupid as well? Drop to your knees, baby angel. I have more power in my little finger than Gabriella and Michelle have in their whole effeminate bodies. So manly. They've never had the courage to look me in the eye. Neither one of them. They flit around behind my back, skirting the edges of humanity, scraping up derelicts like you.

"Do you remember where they found you? In the middle of Manhattan, puking up pus while you licked shit off the sidewalk. Ah, what a grand sight you were. Oh, did I mention that you were married at the time? Abandoned your wife. Not even man enough to stick around during the tough times. But we had fun with her. Twenty of my lackeys got to fuck her to death. The good news is that you don't have to worry about her anymore, as if you ever did.

"Say, how would you like to see her again? She has a history in this building, behind this very desk. She's one of you, but she flies around. You'll have to crawl and beg for the rest of your pathetic life. I'll see to that. But wouldn't it be fun to see the bitch? Talk to her, tell her how sorry you are for the way you treated her?

"Just call her name. Say it with me: 'C-a-t-h-e-r-i-n-e. C-a-t-h-e-r-i-n-e.' Open your jowls, asshole. 'C-a-t-h-e-r-i-n-e.' Start baying like the dog you are. Let her know you're hurting. She'll come gliding in here on those delectable wings."

"That'll be just about enough out of you. In the name of the Father and the Son and the Holy Spirit, we command you to step down!"

"Well look at this, it's the Weanie brothers, Michaela and Gabriella. You couldn't bluff your way out of a cherub's ass, you limp dick morons. I suggest you drop to your knees and beg for mercy."

"You won't impact the bond of two archangels together. We'll continue to protect those who believe in the power of Christ, along with those tormented souls whose salvation lies just beyond their reach."

"You talk platitudes and silly Sunday school slogans. You're worthless, Michael. The power you speak of pales in comparison to mine."

The demon God raised his arms and called forth an army of secondary demons, each of whom appeared to have a serious infection of the mouth. A steady stream of drool secreted from the upper ridges of their multiple tongues, along with a cumulative halitosis that could seemingly move a mountain. Almost as an afterthought, each one appeared to be certifiably insane.

"Holy Spirit of God, send this abomination back into the ground whence it came."

Michael's supplication was answered immediately, as the army of demons melted into dirt beneath his feet. Baal was a little unnerved that it happened so quickly. Michael was obviously not to be bullied.

"We both know she's coming, Michael. That's why you brought little weanie boy with you. What, pray tell, could this scavenger possibly have that would entice a full-fledged angel to come out of hiding? He'll never make it past cadet. You and I both know that. Is he just red meat to satisfy her vampiric cravings?"

Michael had no intention of having this discussion. His assignment was simply to facilitate the arrival of a very special angel, while he protected a very immature cadet in his charge. No one could predict how this would turn out, but two archangels together should be more than capable of holding their position against even the most torrential force of darkness.

Baal knew instinctively that he'd have to separate them quickly if he was to have a chance at a gourmet dinner of virgin angel wings. He was starting to lust for her as well. It was now or never.

Within a split second, the poison from his multiple tongues had begun to sink, deeper and deeper, into the neck of one of the two archangels. A few seconds later, the paralysis was complete. Gabriel could move his eyes and slightly move his wings, but that was about it.

It was now Michael versus the Devil. Michael had no chance, and yet he was overcome with a boundless, overwhelming love that never fails: a love that permeates every cell of our being; every drop of air that we breathe.

"You should have worshiped me, Michael. You would have looked good in that suit and tie. Maybe standing on a street corner, handing out Bibles. You could underline some of your favorite passages, like 'I am the Lord thy God; thou shalt have no other Gods before me.' I would have even autographed them for you."

With that, Baal reached over and crushed Michael's skull between his thumb and forefinger. After pausing for a few moments to enjoy his handiwork, he began to meticulously pluck the eyeballs from Gabriel, who was already near death. With his final breath, Gabriel recalled the words from a song that he heard so long ago: *"Jesus loves me, this I know, for the Bible... tells me..."*

The new cadet was on his knees, beseeching a God he had never known. Both the Devil and his prey could hear the fluttering of wings. It seemed to be coming from a great distance.

"Why does she torture me? I have needs just like she does. If she'll just come to me, I'll take what I need and leave her to bask in my glory. She'll be the Devil's whore."

"She's coming for me, isn't she?"

"Why is that, weanie boy?"

"I don't know. I don't have a clue."

"You angels have a smell. Kind of a bitter, sickly-sweet fragrance that attracts you to each other. God forbid that you should ever fornicate, but He doesn't and you do."

"I just want to get through the night."

"With her on top? I'll tell you what: I'll give you a little boost and start pulling out your fingernails. If you scream loud enough maybe she'll move a little faster."

Both the Devil and his prey were stunned by what appeared to be an apparition that suddenly appeared before them: A beautiful, angelic woman with the most voluptuous wings ever imagined, softly caressing the forehead of the astonished cadet.

"I was lost for so long, David, but I remember everything now. My love affair with music. Baal's henchmen storming into our home, taking our beautiful daughter from us. And she was beautiful, David. Innocent, beautiful, and happy. We watched her being mauled and mutilated. At six years old.

"I could never blame you for falling apart. No father on earth could have held up after that. I knew you were in the gutter, but I had nothing left to give, for I was demolished as well."

Baal started to applaud. "Nice speech. Wow, I'm impressed."

"I'm taking him with me. You'll never be able to touch him again. This is my promise to him and to my God. In the name of the Father, and the Son, and the Holy Spirit, I command you to step down!"

As Baal tried to move toward her, Catherine thrust out her right hand with the palm open. Baal screamed with pain as his forehead became inflamed with a heavenly fire more concentrated and powerful than even the Devil's inferno. The fire from her hand continued to rage throughout the night as she stood her ground, with the new cadet cowering behind her. Baal, in extreme pain and unable to move, remained undeterred.

"Time means nothing to me. You're weak. You'll tire. I won't."

"A man who loves me once rose from the dead. Time means nothing to me either."

"Cheap magician's tricks. Water into wine, walking on water, raising the dead. What has he ever done for you?"

"He brought me here."

"I brought you here, you little bitch!"

With that, Baal made his one and only mistake: In anger, he blinked. During that dark, infinitesimal pause, his supposed conquests simply disappeared. For it's widely known that the Devil often stumbles when he's challenged with the certainty of God's promise, for he suffers from a monumental inferiority complex.

Catherine found herself enmeshed in a very disturbing dream. She was perched high on a roof with David by her side. It was time for them to jump. She kept trying to get his attention, but he looked right through her.

"Let him go, Catherine. He's not ready yet."

She turned to greet the mysterious, comforting voice. It belonged to a man dressed in a white robe, a man who seemed strangely familiar. He was studying Catherine with a faint look of amusement.

"We've lost two of our best, Catherine. Raphael will take over, with Uriel as second in command, but I need you to step in immediately. Raphael is the great healer. He and

Uriel will be out of circulation indefinitely until they've had time to assess the damage caused to our two greatest warriors. In the meantime, you'll be in charge."

"But… why me?"

"The question I want you to think about is, 'Why not me?'"

Catherine suddenly found herself awake and alone in the middle of Manhattan, on the roof of a building similar to the one in which she had once lived. As she balanced on the edge, with her memories now intact, she remembered the moment when her life changed forever, the moment when she stepped into the abyss.

"Would I do it again?" she wondered.

"Go ahead, do it again," was the Devil's reply. "I'll caress you as you fall from the sky. I'll make love to you on the hood of a broken-down taxi. For I, Lucifer; I, Mephistopheles; I, Baal; I, Satan, am your true love, your true Master."

As Catherine carefully unfolded her gigantic wings, the incredible beauty of life itself overwhelmed her senses. He doesn't understand, she thought. He'll never understand. The man in the white robe was her one true love, her true Master. In the blink of an eye, she began to ascend, upward and outward into the night.

THE END

The Secret to Happiness

You don't have a clue, do you. You think I'm just like all the others: timid, weak, willing to beg for scraps from any poor slob who stoops to throw me a bone. But I'm telling you, it's not like that. My shingle is an honorable shingle.

I survived the years of bone-crushing poverty, staggering through the shadows of opportunity with my hand clenched tightly around a Johnny Walker Black. But just a few moments ago, some great, liberating force managed to pry my eyes open, and there it was: the secret to happiness, buried deep within the terrors of my own mind.

I'd share it with you… really, I would… but I don't think you'd see it. It's too damn obvious. But, look… you're probably starting to think I'm crazy anyway. So, what the hell, let's give it a shot.

This great force just revealed to me, and I mean <u>just</u> revealed to me (I was dozing off, with my head on my desk), that we're all on the path to happiness, but the path is littered with our own broken-down bodies: some standing, some lying, some squatting. Once in a while somebody walks past, going somewhere. We don't even bother to nod. It's none of our business.

You see what I'm saying? We never go anywhere. We just accept what we appear to be. That's the tragedy of the whole thing. By accepting what we appear to be, we're ignoring what we really are.

The secret to happiness, according to this great force, is simply to forget and move on. Yesterday's rose is today's junk heap. Find a new rose. There are plenty of them up ahead, but you'll never find one unless you start walking.

O.K., I'm babbling. I disappointed you, didn't I. You thought I might have been on to something. Well, all I can say is there's… Jesus, holy shit! I know, I know, I'm edgy as hell.

How high did I jump, anyway? If I were you, I'd just kind of move over in that direction a little bit, so you're out of the line of fire. Just in case. Hold on a second, I'll get it.

Ah, it was just the janitor telling me he wanted to go home early. I told him he could kiss my ass.

You know something? I gotta laugh. The poor guy's probably scared out of his pants, and all he can tell me is he wants to go home. He can't bring himself to ask what the bodies are doing out there. Blood plastered all over the place. Jesus.

Look, man, it's been a long day. I'm just sitting here trying to figure it all out. You got a minute? Let's have a drink. You know, this started out like any other day. I was knocking down a bourbon and coke at about ten, ten thirty this morning when somebody started knocking on the door. Now, keep in mind, nobody knocks on my door. Nobody had knocked on my door in over a month. Here you go, I hope you like bourbon. So, I thought I must be dreaming.

You see, a little over a month ago I started locking the door during business hours. Now, don't look at me like that. I know some people are going to see the door's locked and probably figure I'm closed. But if they don't bother to knock, so the fuck what? What difference does it make?

You want a little more coke in that? You O.K.? You're not a very animated type guy, are you. So anyway, as I was saying, I keep the door locked during business hours. Yeah, I know I get a little defensive about it. It's just that I like to have a little nip now and then, and sometimes I fall asleep at my desk.

But you know, I felt good about answering the door this morning. I really did. Sometimes you need somebody real to talk to. Like you, for example. So, I sauntered over to the door like it was the most natural thing in the world.

"Yes?"

What can I say? She was beyond beautiful. She was fall-down, knock-you-out-of-your-shorts beautiful. Thirty-two, thirty-three, maybe a little older. Pouty lips. Elongated neck. Prominent cheek bones. Tough. Used to getting her way. And, oh yes… scared to death.

"Are you Mr. Logan?"

"This dream just keeps getting better and better. Yeah, I'm Logan. Come on in."

She took about three steps inside, then stopped. "Mr. Logan, I don't… I don't know if I'm going to be able to get through this. I came to you because I couldn't think of anybody else to turn to."

I walked over to my desk and poured myself a little confidence-builder. Of course, being a gentleman, I offered her one as well. She declined with a wave of her hand, as if the very suggestion had offended her. So, I leaned back against my desk and released a rather overwhelming belch. She was not amused.

"Mr. Logan, are you in any condition to help me?"

"What? You mean this? This is just something to pass the time. I can take it or leave it."

"Then will you please leave it for a moment so I can talk to you?"

"All right, I'll listen. Go ahead. Amuse me. I haven't heard a good sob story in a long time. But before you start… Why me?"

"Paul Killian once spoke highly of you."

"Paul Killian? Where?"

"He's my husband." The tears started to flow, quietly and copiously. I couldn't help feeling that she was worse off than I ever was, so I handed her my bourbon and coke. She handed it back. "Mr. Logan, please don't torture me this way."

"O.K., I'll tell you what…" I reached out with my foot and shoved a chair up in front of the desk. "You sit here, I'll sit behind my desk, and we'll pretend that I know what the fuck I'm doing. You pretend that I'm 'King Shit of Private Eye Land,' and I'll pretend that I'm really good at what I do. Or used to do."

"Mr. Logan, don't you need to make a living? I can afford to pay you."

"It's too late. I'm pulling my shingle. My landlord has a bug up his ass. Thinks I'm an undesirable or something. And if Paul Killian wants to see me, why doesn't he just send a couple of his thugs?"

"He doesn't even know you exist. You're an insignificant flea in his universe. I know you were friends once, but that was a long time ago."

"He told you we were friends?"

"I suppose he did. But with all due respect, Mr. Logan, you haven't exactly set the world on fire the last few years. They laugh at you, Mr. Logan. Everybody laughs at you. I'm not saying this to hurt you. It's just that I don't have time to stroke your besotted ego. We need each other, Mr. Logan. I can help you with your finances, and you can help me stay alive.

"There'll be a hefty bonus for you, above and beyond your normal fees, if you can just expose the identity of my husband's lover. I have reason to believe he may be hiding her in our home, perhaps even in our bedroom. Of course, I'll need substantial proof. Pictures, what have you. And Mr. Logan... this has to be wrapped up within the next twenty-four hours."

"Twenty-four hours? Nothing happens in twenty-four hours. It's impossible."

"Then I'll be dead, Mr. Logan, and you'll be broke. Mr. Logan, I've lived a very fortunate life until now. I've never needed anyone, but I need you. I'll pay you anything you want."

The broad started to look a little light-headed. I thought she was going to throw up. Instead, she swooned right in front of me.

Great, I thought. Looks like one of my old scams. The old "faint in the office" routine. Get him to carry you somewhere... anywhere. At the moment of truth put your arms around him, reach up and plant the most passionate kiss on record. Snap, snap. Done.

Scare the stupid son-of-a-bitch into complying with something essentially harmless. Strictly small-time stuff. It's not that big a deal to give us what we want compared with the slight chance that his wife might actually believe these cheesy pictures. It's quick, nobody gets hurt, and I make enough to go out and have a couple beers and a steak.

So, what the hell should I do with her? Paul Killian's wife… Christ! I'm supposed to go up against that insane bastard just to get some naughty pictures for his wife?

I looked down at her, sprawled out on the floor, her skirt crawling half way up her thighs. I have to admit I was highly aroused. This was one great looking broad. I wanted to reach down and tear the buttons off her blouse one by one. Instead, I gently picked her up in my arms. For lack of a better idea, I decided to lay her flat on the top of my desk.

She started to moan these little moans. That aroused me even more. Then she started to squirm around on the desk. Finally, her eyes opened barely enough to recognize me.

"What… what happened?" she slurred.

"You made a pass at me."

Her body shot up to a sitting position. "What?"

"You fainted. I didn't know what else to do with you."

"Mr. Logan… my life is in danger. Don't you have any compassion for me?"

"How long have you been married to Genghis Khan?"

"Married? Did I say we were married? It's not quite like that."

"How exactly is it?"

"He adopted me when I was fourteen. I became his mistress when I was sixteen. You might say he created me, Mr. Logan. Everything I am, I learned through him. We lived together as man and wife until about three weeks ago when he locked me in a small bedroom in the mansion. I haven't seen him since."

"How did you get out?"

"I begged the servant who brought me my food to let me get some air. I'm afraid now that I did a foolish thing. He'll surely kill her when he finds out. I walked the streets all night until I thought of you."

"Was this servant somebody you trusted?"

"I didn't really know her. She was new."

"Christ, she was a plant. He was testing you. He just wanted to see what you'd do."

"But nobody followed me."

"Of course, somebody followed you. They're reporting to Genghis as we speak."

"No! He'll kill me."

"If he wants you dead, do you really think I can protect you?"

"The pictures, Mr. Logan. Get me pictures. It's the only chance I have."

"It's not enough. You have to go to the police."

"He owns the police. He is the police. Help me, Mr. Logan."

"Open the door. It's a fairly busy corridor at this time of day. Just tell me if there's anybody you recognize out there."

She slithered off the desk and stuck her long neck out into the hallway. After a few seconds she pulled it back in and shut the door. Her face had turned ashen.

"Two of his killers are leaning against the wall down the hallway. One of them waved at me."

"Nice touch. Was he grinning?"

"From ear to ear."

"You sure there're just two of them?"

"Yes, I know them well. They're evil."

"Well, I'm going to go light a candle up their ass. Go hide under my desk. If anything happens to me, just start praying. This is the only way out."

I opened the door, pasted a big smile on my face, and walked quickly toward the two gorillas. One of them stiffened and put his hand inside his coat. He looked like a nasty fuck all right. The other one just kept leaning back against the wall, seemingly bored to death. I went for the stiff one.

"Paul Killian's on the phone. I've known Paul for over thirty years. Did he ever tell you we were roommates in college? Come on in, guys. Paul says you're not much, but you're the best he's got. He wants you to take the little lady back in one piece. Says he's got big plans for her. And another thing… he says don't fuck it up, just do as he says."

I started walking back toward my office. The fuckers hadn't budged. "Hurry it up, guys. You don't keep Paul Killian waiting. Let's get this over with." I stopped at the door and looked back. The gorillas kept looking at each other, at me, at each other, at me.

Finally, they started walking toward the door. I stepped inside, braced myself, and gathered the force of hell into my right fist. As the first one walked in, I nailed him with a shot to the throat. The brass knuckles helped. Got him good. He'll probably never talk again, other than maybe a whisper. But a stiff like that only knows about ten words he can use anyway. So, fuck him.

The other gorilla drew his gun and crouched down in the hallway outside my door, ready for action. He didn't look bored anymore. A few people were out in the hallway, so he knew he had to do something quick. These guys are trained not to call attention to themselves. I stayed out of sight, next to the door. Bozo was still on the floor, bleeding from the mouth. "Hey! Hey!" the dummy outside called out. "What's going on in there?" I kept quiet.

"Hey! Just send out the girl. Give me the girl and I'll leave." Again, no response. So, he stood up and ran down the hallway into the stairwell. Then Bozo got up and ran out the door and down the hallway. I had his gun.

"Bravo, Mr. Logan. That was masterful." She was applauding as she came up from under the desk.

"Just get the hell out of here. They'll be back."

"Are you going to help me, Mr. Logan?"

"I'll think about it. I just can't see why these pictures are so goddamned important. This isn't about pictures. Pictures are for divorce cases, blackmail, chicken-shit stuff. Why does this smell like something a hell of a lot more devious? You're going for his jugular, aren't you."

"I'm fighting for my life, Mr. Logan."

"No, it's more than that. This reeks of payback. You want to bring the bastard to his knees more than you want to live. You want to cut his balls off. I'm not even sure he knows what you're up to. Maybe I should get his side of it."

"Mr. Logan, he's going to kill me unless you can perform a miracle. These pictures are my only hope. You have a reputation for lugging your camera with you everywhere. Why don't you call him and see if you can get an invitation to the mansion. After what you did to his ace killer, he'll want to see what makes you tick. He admires anybody who can beat him in battle, as long as he wins the war."

"Great. Why don't you get him on the phone. Tell him I miss him so much I get all weepy-eyed. I'd like to come over so I can kiss his ass."

"It'll be much better if you call him, Mr. Logan. Get the invitation and I'll tell you everything you need to know about the mansion, including the location of the master bedroom. You're welcome to kiss his ass for all I care. Your job is to get the pictures and then get out of there alive."

"For Christ's sake, what are the odds on that? I'm just going to waltz in there and start walking around the hallways, opening doors wherever I want?"

"The door to our bedroom will be locked. I assume he'll have guards out in front. One of them may be your Mr. Bozo."

"What?"

"Isn't that what you called him?"

"Christ, what an airhead."

"They're coming back for me, Mr. Logan, you said it yourself. This isn't the time to make fun of me. Please do as I ask before it's too late."

"Why exactly does he want you dead?"

Here came the sniffles again. "He's bored with me."

"And…?"

"And I think he's scared of me."

"You know too much?"

"Yes."

"I guess that means he'll have to kill me if I get these pictures."

"I have my own bank accounts, Mr. Logan. I can pay you more money than you've ever dreamed of. Think about it, Mr. Logan. What are the alternatives? Abject poverty? Alcoholism?"

"I'll need twenty thousand dollars up front."

"All right, I'll write you a check."

"Go get me twenty thousand in cash. Just to make the call."

"You know that won't be possible, not on such short notice."

"Why don't you open your purse and we'll see if it's possible. I bet there's a lot more than twenty thousand in there. Lay the twenty on me and I'll make the call."

She pulled a nine-millimeter out of her purse and pointed it at my crotch. "I'll give you ten thousand to make the call, Mr. Logan. But if you don't do it right, I may want it back."

"Sure, baby. That'll get us to the next step. Just put it in my hand."

"I'd like to put it in your hand, Mr. Logan, but I'm afraid you wouldn't know what to do with it. From what I hear, you haven't had much of it in your hand recently. Suppose I just set it on the desk like this, and you can pick it up after the phone call."

Stacks of hundreds suddenly appeared on my desk. After a quick glance, I realized it was a hell of a lot less than ten thousand. The scheming broad had laced the hundreds with singles. I told her to go get the rest.

I guess I should've just made the call and let it go at that. I could buy a few things with six thousand bucks. Maybe a decent suit. My shoes have got holes in them. My socks… forget about it. I changed my underwear last week. I think it was on Thursday.

Hey, I get by. I told her I needed the money because she's putting my life in danger. But, come on. Is my life really worth twenty thousand dollars? I doubt it. What is any life worth? A million dollars? Fifty thousand? I should just take the six thousand and go buy a decent pair of shoes. If I have to go to the mansion, you know I'm going to get whacked anyway. I'm thinking I should just have it out with them right here. This office is my mansion. Let 'em come to me. That gives me the edge.

Reach over there and drop a couple ice cubes in this, will you? Thanks. All right, where was I? All right, now it's getting to be late in the afternoon and I'm starting to think it's kind of sad about the broad. She really believes these pictures are going to save her life. From my perspective the only thing that's going to save her life is to get the old man out of the house and let me whack him.

I'm tired of dragging that fuckin' camera around with me. I'm thinking I gotta play this smart. Take control of the situation. When she gets back with the rest of the money, I'll put her under wraps. Make it so nobody can get to her for a few days while I try to sort this out.

Then all of a sudden, I hear this familiar voice outside in the hall. "Hey, Chris! Unlock the door. It's Paul."

"Paul! What took you so long? It's been over thirty years."

"I know, Chris. Open the door. I want to have a look at you."

"I don't think I want to do that, Paul. Maybe you should call for an appointment."

"Come on, Chris. You were always a joker. Never serious about anything. Come on, open the door. We've got a lot of catching up to do."

"I don't think that's a good idea, Paul. Why don't you just keep shouting through the door. I can hear you just fine."

"The problem with that, Chris, is that everybody else in the damn building can hear me too. Come on. Open the door."

"You turned out to be a prick, Paul. I always throw the pricks out anyway."

"You're such a joker, Chris. The same old Chris. Remember when we used to kick ass together down on the waterfront... all those sleazy cocksuckers. It seems like yesterday, doesn't it. But I'll tell you, when things got really rough, we'd always stick you out in front.

"You were a hell of an enforcer in those days. It looks like you still got it, Chris. Jesus, what did you hit this poor guy with? He can't talk. Nothing comes out but a whisper. I don't even want him around me anymore. It gives me the creeps."

"I'm glad he's doing well."

"You gotta come to work for me, Chris. Nobody has your balls and your smarts. Come on. Open the damn door."

"Where are you standing, Paul?"

"What?"

"I'm going to fire through the fucking door. Maybe you ought to move or duck or something."

"You're a crazy cocksucker, aren't you. They say you're a washed-up, wet-brain, weak-willed son-of-a-bitch. Why don't you just stick the bullet in your brain. Save me the trouble."

"It's no trouble for you, Paul. I used to rough those guys up because it was my job. You came behind me and tortured and killed the poor bastards just for the fun of it."

"You're weak, Chris. That's why you're a drunk. Nobody else could've built an empire like mine. You bet I was tough. I had to let 'em know they couldn't fuck with me. Kind of like you're fucking with me now."

"No, Paul, I'm not the one fucking with you. Your little mistress wife, or whatever the fuck she is… that's the one who's fucking with you. She's going to take a big bite out of your balls, and I'm going to enjoy every minute of it."

"You're going to make me keep shouting, aren't you Chris. It's embarrassing. I'm a very important man in this town, Chris. Now open the fucking door."

"Why don't you open it, Paul?" I moved over to the side of the door, against the wall, with my gun pointed at the door. From there I reached over and released the lock.

"Now, you're not going to do anything stupid, are you Chris? I just came here to talk to you. This broad is fucking with your brain. We need to talk this out. It's not what you think it is."

"Come in alone. Leave the girls outside. I don't want to have to look at that whispering fucker."

"All right, Chris, if that's what you want. Just take it easy. I just want to talk to you."

The door opened slowly. I gotta tell you, the years had not been kind. I always thought he was an ugly son-of-a-bitch, with those pockmarks and skinny lips. Now he was bald and bloated. His toupee looked like a giant piece of lint, hanging on for dear life.

"See, that wasn't so bad, was it Chris. You're paranoid, man. You think your old friend is here to whack you. That's bullshit, man. You and I go back a long way. I don't whack my friends, Chris. My friends all work for me."

"Let's cut the crap. Shut the door and lock it. Then tell me about the broad."

"You're giving me orders, Chris? That's funny. Nobody gives me orders. Under any other circumstances, I'd..."

"Here's one for you, Paul. Bend over and grab your ankles so you can kiss your own ass, you lying cocksucker. Just don't expect me to pucker up and join in. Now tell me your side of it, then get the fuck out of here."

"You should learn to relax, Chris. Your temper was always your downfall."

"Tell me about the broad."

"She's crazy as a loon. I put up with her because she's great in bed. What else can I tell you? She's a crazy, fucking broad."

"Crazy how?"

"She's delusional. She sees things. She hears things. Hey, Chris, I ain't no angel. I've got a lot of broads on the side. But she thinks I've got one stashed away in my bedroom. That's sick. I ain't about to violate the sanctity of my home and my marriage."

"Your marriage?"

"How much has she told you, Chris?"

"Why did you lock her in a room?"

"To protect her from herself, I guess. I didn't know what to do with her. I don't want to put her in one of those nut houses. You gotta believe me, I still love the broad. I just don't want her to get hurt. I'm trying to protect her."

"What a crock. You think I'm a fool, Paul?"

"You're a fool if you get sucked into her story. If she acts like she's scared it's because she's going insane. I feel sorry for her."

"Who do you have stashed away, Paul?"

"Nobody. You're a skeptical son-of-a-bitch, aren't you. You think you'd believe your old friend before you'd hitch up with this dame."

A soft knock on the door broke the tension somewhat. "Chris, I'm just going to check this out. I asked my men to let me know if they see something suspicious."

He opened the door, then quickly started groping his way backwards, very rigidly and awkwardly, like a duck in heat. I didn't see the broad at first. She had a gun pressed tightly into his genitals.

"Were you expecting me, sweetie?"

"Please, honey, don't do this. Let's just go home. You got nothing to worry about. I'll take good care of you this time. But, baby, how did you get past my men?"

"Oh, come on, lover. Haven't you ever heard of a silencer? You always said you haven't lived until your lover shoves his cold, hard steel up against your crotch. This is the one you used to make me suck."

"Please, baby, not here. It's time for us to go home. We can talk it out on the way home.

"Just give daddy the gun now. C'mon, sweetheart. Daddy will take care of everything. Just give me the gun."

Funny thing, but that's exactly what she did. Instead of blowing his balls off she just handed him the gun. Then she just meekly stood there while he backed up and peeked out into the hallway. She looked like a little girl, waiting to be told that everything was O.K.

"Well, you whacked 'em, didn't you baby. There's nobody else out here. I guess we're okay." He turned to me. "Just forget you ever saw us, Chris. If the police question you, you didn't hear anything. She used a silencer."

They started to leave. Believe me, I couldn't think of any reason to object. He had her tight by the arm, but she pulled away and started walking toward me. "Go ahead, I'll catch up. I need a minute with Mr. Logan." She walked right up to me and looked me in the eyes. She got real close and stared at me for a few seconds, then she stuck an envelope in my hand. "Here, keep this for a rainy day."

'Daddy' was getting frantic. "What the hell are you doing? Goddamn it, what's going on?"

"I promised Mr. Logan a little something for his trouble. It's only fair. After all, I hired him to do a job for me."

"Well, he won't be doing any more jobs in this town. Now let's get the fuck out of here."

But the broad wasn't through with me yet. She got right up in my face and started rubbing her tongue along the edge of my lips. "Umm. Why don't you just run along without me. Three weeks is way too long for a girl to be locked up. I think it's my turn to have some fun."

I gotta tell you, this didn't seem like fun to me. I could see the headline in tomorrow's paper: 'Genghis Khan castrates obscure private eye for fooling around with his nut-case wife.'

"You gotta get out of here," I said. "If you don't move now, it's gonna be too late. Get out while you can."

But she wasn't about to leave. Instead, she threw her arms around me and gave me the biggest, wettest, deepest kiss I've ever had. I tried to pull back but, come on, I didn't really want it to end. Ever.

Loverboy ran over to us and grabbed her by the hair. She squealed and turned on him with a vengeance, wildly flailing her arms in all directions. I had to laugh. She really nailed him a couple times. He got a bloody nose and probably a hell of a shiner. Somehow, he managed to get her out the door.

I looked out into the hallway. It was early in the evening. Everybody in the building had gone home, except maybe the janitors. Nobody was out there except the two stiffs.

Boy, this dame is a stone killer. One of the stiffs was lying at the end of the hallway with half his head blown off. The other was in the middle of the hallway, two doors down from mine. It looked like he might have had time to pull out his gun, but that was about it. The barrel of his gun had been stuffed inside his mouth.

I took one look and decided to just leave it alone. I'll say I didn't hear anything. Who's to know the difference? Nobody in this building pays any attention to anybody else anyway. They all live in their own little…

Christ, here we go again. Something tells me it's not the janitor this time. You got a gun? This is the third floor… you're not going anywhere unless you go through that door. What the fuck's wrong with you, anyway? You don't say anything, you don't do anything, you just sit there and stare at me. I'm trying to keep you out of trouble, man. Are you packin' or not?

"Open the fuckin' door, Chris. We're going to play this out. You might as well open the door and take it like a man."

"Did you miss me, Paul? Long time no see. How's your adorable wife? Great liplock, Paul. Did she ever play the trombone?"

"Nobody humiliates me like that and lives to tell about it. I slit her throat in the elevator on the way out of here."

Jesus! I gotta sit down. Why are you shaking your head no? This guy's a ruthless son-of-a-bitch. He doesn't care about his wife or anybody else. He's all about power. Of course, he killed her.

"Funny thing, though. I get home and I see that she's ransacked my bedroom. Then I notice something important missing. Something real important. Can you tell me, Chris? Can you tell me what's missing?"

"Pictures."

"Then you've got 'em. That's what she handed you in the envelope."

"Wait a minute. She handed me money in the envelope."

"Did you open the envelope?"

"Not yet, Paul. But you've got me goddamn curious. You really think it's pictures?"

"You've got one chance to walk out of here alive, Chris. Shove the fuckin' envelope under the door. If I see the seal's broken, I'm going to have to kill you. If the seal hasn't been broken, I'll let you walk."

"I think I might want to enjoy these pictures. Hell, if it's not money I can't go anywhere and spend it. I might as well just put my feet up and enjoy an evening of entertainment. Pictures, huh? I wonder who I can invite to share these with. Hmm… hey, I got it. The editor of the Times. Might as well share it with the whole fuckin' world."

"Let me ask you one question, Chris. If you haven't opened the envelope, how did you know about the pictures?"

"The most beautiful woman I've ever seen seemed to think they could save her life. Funny thing, though… I don't think she wanted to use them. I think she loved you. You wouldn't know about love, though, would you Paul."

"She's the only one I've ever loved, you fuckin' idiot. Slip the envelope under the door or say your fuckin' prayers. I'm not going to wait for your pussy-ass to play this goddamn game through the door with me."

"Hey, Paul, where are the police? You could've had a whole battalion of dirty cops down here to finish me off. Why are you playing the Lone Ranger all of a sudden? Wait, let me guess. If anybody sees these pictures and lives to tell about it… well, you can take it from there. Must be some pretty fuckin' heavy stuff in this envelope. I guess it's time for me to have a peek. Shit!"

"Well, that solves the problem of the locked door. Gee, Chris, your door's got a big hole in it. And, what do you know… there's a big hole in you, too. I hope it was worth it, Chris. I hope you got an eyeful.

"Chris, listen to me. I know you're dying, but I'm still gonna have to blow your face off. Closed casket all the way. But, fuck, who the hell's going to come to your funeral anyway?

"What, Chris? Let me get down here on the floor and you can try to tell me. God, that's a lot of blood you're coughing up. It's a shame it had to end like this. So, what are you trying to tell me, Chris? Who's going to come to your funeral?"

"He…"

"He? He's going to come to your funeral? There's nobody here, Chris. You're all alone on this one, buddy. Oh, by the way, I didn't kill my wife. I just gave her a sedative. She's home sleeping. I get to fuck her when I get home. Who do you get to fuck, Chris? What's that? Speak up, Chris, you're slobbering in your blood. You? What do you mean, you?"

"Fuck you."

"Chris, Chris, such negative talk from a man who's got, oh, about thirty seconds left to live. You know, Chris, you're a standup guy. Look at this. The seal on the envelope was never broken. You never violated my trust in you. I'm touched. But what are friends for, anyway?

"So, what are you trying to say, Chris? Spit it out. Secret? Is that what you said? I bet you want to know what these pictures are all about. Shit, Chris, if I told you that I'd have to kill you. Oh, that's right, I already did."

"Secret…"

"All right, Chris, I guess it wouldn't hurt anything for a friend to share a secret with a friend. This is the last thing you're going…"

"Happiness."

"Good, I'm glad you're happy about it. I don't think you can see anymore, Chris, so I'll whisper it in your ear. You'll love this, Chris. You'll understand why I've never told this to anyone before. My world would come crashing down if this got out. I'd be a laughingstock. You see, I took most of these pictures myself, but I got to be in a couple of them. They're for my eyes only.

"Here it is, Chris. I'll give you about five seconds to let it soak in, then I'm going to blow your fuckin' head off. Here it is. I'll get right down here and lay this in your ear. Are you ready?

"I'm gay as a fruitcake. Always have been. Remember all that tongue you devoured earlier today? Hope you enjoyed it, baby, 'cause here's the good part. My wife's got a pecker.

"She's a boy, Chris. I just dressed him up so nobody knew. Au revoir, motherfucker."

"Fuck, did you have to splatter on my clothes, Chris? You lived too long for a maggot anyway. I did the world a favor by… what the fuck? Who the fuck are you? Answer me, you son-of-a-bitch. Who the fuck are you? Don't touch me. What are you doing? I can't get up. I can't get up.

"You son-of-a-bitch, what did you do to me? I don't want to die like this. Help me, for Christ's sake, don't just stare at me. Ahh… it fuckin' hurts. Why did you have to touch me? What do you mean, 'find a new rose,' you grim motherfucker. Help me. Please…"

"So, what have you got, Harry?"

"It looks like a couple fags knocked each other off. Pretty sick. One of them was lying on top of the other one. We've got gay, nude porno pictures in an envelope. It looks like one of them was trying to blackmail the other one."

"Anybody we know?"

"You might as well leave, Charlie. No pictures and no story. The guy renting this office was one Christopher A. Logan, a private eye known for just scraping the bottom of the barrel. A sleazebag. He's got no family and, apparently, no friends."

"How about the other one?"

"Ah, just some lowlife creep. Nothing here of any consequence. I'm going to wrap it up quickly. Why don't we get together at the end of your shift for coffee and some breakfast. I'll meet you at the diner at, let's say, midnight."

"Okay, Harry. But can't I get a look at the bodies?"

"Nah, they're going to bury this thing. We don't want to glorify these faggots by putting their pictures in the paper. Just let it go, Charlie. Why don't you get out there and find a real story. Something that'll be of interest to your readers. Sorry, Charlie, I gotta go. Give my love to Louise.

"All right, I got rid of him. Now let's get the bodies out of here. Is the ambulance out in front? Good. That's just for show, of course, in case somebody walks by. Tom, keep those bodies covered whatever you do. And, Tom, has Mrs. Killian been notified? You better get on it.

"Try to break it to her gently, 'cause she's going to take this hard. A beautiful, loving wife like that. She doesn't have to know that her husband was a fag. Are we agreed on that? God, did you see those pictures? It makes you sick to your stomach. But we worked for this man. We all did. He took good care of us. Nobody's going to deny that. Right?

"Here's the official story, then. Governor Killian died late this evening of a massive heart attack. His lovely wife, Natalie, was by his side at their home in the Governor's Mansion. Tom, you'll have to clear this with her. Tell her he was out with the boys, having a few drinks. But we thought it would look better, officially, if he died at home with his wife. Got it?"

"Wait a minute, Harry. Take a look at this picture. You ain't gonna believe it."

"I'm not gonna look at any more of this filth. Seeing the Governor with a hard-on isn't exactly my idea of a good time. Just burn 'em. All of 'em. Get rid of 'em before anybody else sees 'em."

"Just look at this one, boss. I'm telling you; you won't believe it."

"Oh, for Christ's sake, give it to me. What the…? Holy shit. Holy Christ Almighty. It's Mrs. Killian, isn't it. Or should I call her Mister Killian."

"Fuckin' 'A,' you should."

"Tommy, my boy, can you keep a secret?"

"I think so, boss."

"We got something here the whole world would like to get their hands on. Information like this, Tommy? Shit. This is power beyond belief. If we let this out the whole organization would crumble. Nobody's gonna want to align himself with something like this. It'll be the biggest scandal in history."

"What are you gettin' at, boss?"

"Get Mrs. Killian on the phone. Then get me Chief Ramsey. I think you and I are about ready for a promotion."

"I kind of like the way you're talkin,' boss."

"This will be our secret, Tommy. We'll use it only if we have to. We just gotta let a few key people know that we got it."

"I can't believe it, boss. We just stumbled onto the secret to…"

"Happiness?"

"Yeah, boss, I like that. The secret to happiness."

"Tommy, who the hell is that over there in the corner?"

"I don't know. Forensics?"

"Hey! What the fuck are you doing over there? If you're through with your work get the hell out of here."

"Jesus!"

"What the …?"

"Did you see what I saw, boss?"

"I don't know what the hell I saw. I think this moron just ate his own eyeball. It rolled down his face and he ate it."

"I saw him do it, boss."

"Well, what are you waiting for? Go arrest him."

"For what?"

"I don't know… mayhem. Anything."

"Shit, boss…"

"I know, I saw it too. He just ate his lips. Let's get the fuck out of here."

"Where's the door? Where's the fuckin' door?"

"Shit! There is no door."

"I'm gettin' dizzy, boss. Fuck. Look at this place. Where are we? It's just a bunch of dead fuckin' roses. Everywhere. Rotten, stinking roses!"

"I can see into the next room, Tommy. Look!"

"It ain't the next room, boss. It's this room. It's Mrs. Killian. It looks like she's using a silencer. Fuck, I can see the bullet coming straight at me. It's gonna hit me right between the eyes."

"Where are we, Tommy? Everything's moving in slow motion. I think we walked into hell. Mrs. Killian with a gun and a dick? Yeah, it's hell all right."

"Now this fucker's trying to eat my eyeball. Get him off me, boss! Get him the hell off me!"

"It's too late, Tommy!"

"Boss... Ahhhhhhhhhhh!"

"Au revoir, motherfucker. C'est la vie."

THE END

www.ingramcontent.com/pod-product-compliance
Lightning Source LLC
Chambersburg PA
CBHW061347140726
47997CB00003B/1090